This Book Belongs To:

....

This edition published by Parragon Books Ltd in 2017 and distributed by

Parragon Inc.
440 Park Avenue South, 13th Floor
New York, NY 10016
www.parragon.com

Copyright © Parragon Books Ltd. 2013–2017

Text © Hollins University

Written by Margaret Wise Brown
Illustrated by Henry Fisher

Edited by Michael Diggle
Designed by Ailsa Cullen
Production by Jonathan Wakeham

ISBN 978-1-4748-9973-4

Printed in China

The **Fish** with the Deep-Sea **Smile**

PaRragon

Bath · New York · Cologne · Melbourne · Delhi
Hong Kong · Shenzhen · Singapore

They fished
and they fished,

Way down in the sea,

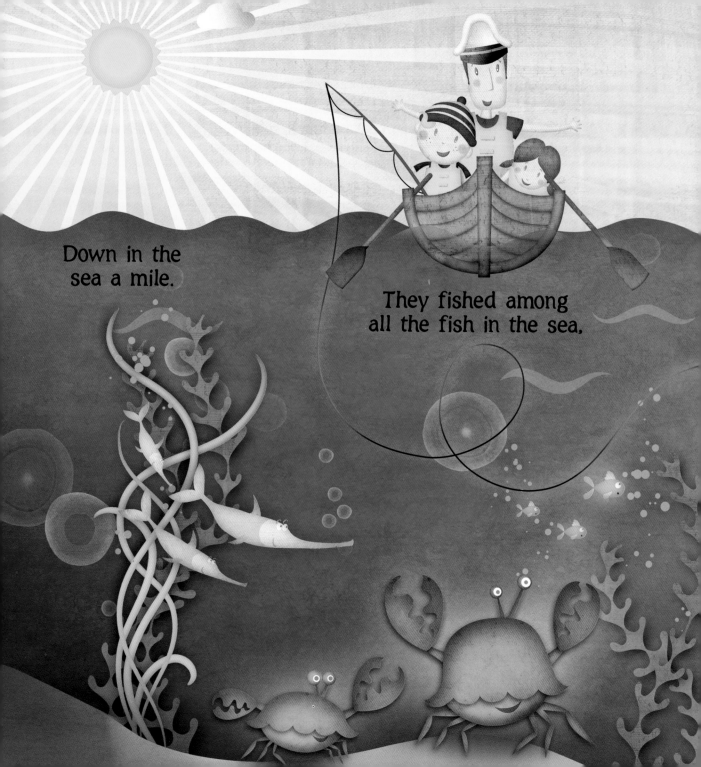

Down in the
sea a mile.

They fished among
all the fish in the sea,

For the fish with the
deep-sea smile.

One fish came up
from the deep of the sea,

From down in the sea a mile.
It had blue-green eyes
and whiskers three,
But never a deep-sea smile.

One fish came up
from the deep of the sea,
From down in the sea a mile,

With electric lights
up and down its tail,
But never a deep-sea smile.

They fished
and they fished,
All across the sea,

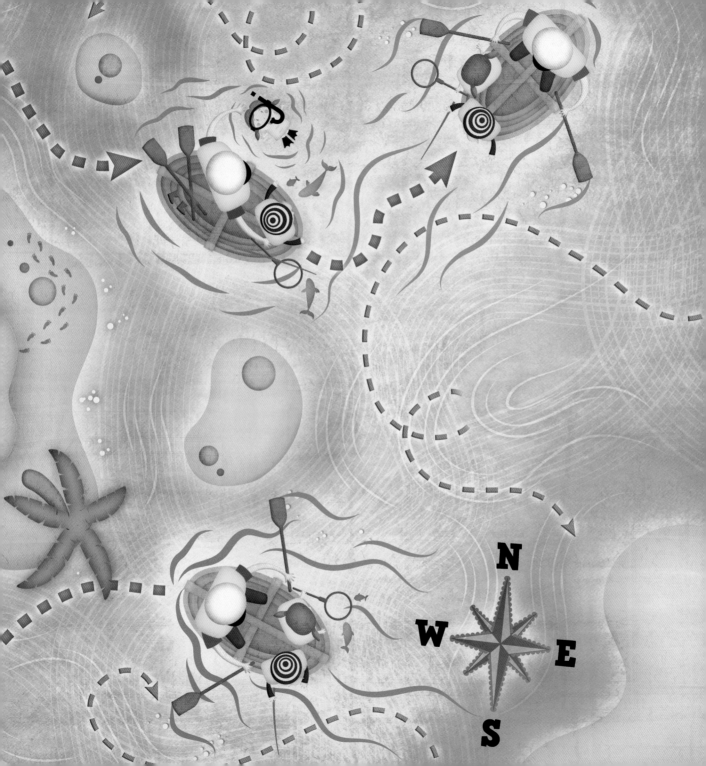

And down in the depths a mile.
They fished among all the fish in the sea,

For the fish with
the deep-sea smile.

One fish came up with
terrible teeth.

One fish with a long, strong jaw.

One fish came up with eyes on stalks,

One fish with terrible claws.

They fished all through the ocean deep,
For many and many a mile.

And then, one day,
they got a pull,

From down in the
sea a mile.

And when they pulled
the fish into the boat,

He smiled a
deep-sea smile.

And as he smiled, the hook got free,
And then, what a deep-sea smile!

He flipped his tail and
swam away,

Down in the sea a mile.